Woody's
Roundup
Hey
Howdy
Hey!
Woody's
Roundup
Ages 6 to 10
WOODY'S
ROPIN' RODEO
GAME
Hey howdy hey!
Let's play!
500
200
LASSO TARGET

ISBN: 0-7172-8988-5

Published by Grolier Books, a division of Grolier Enterprises, Inc.

Disney · PIXAR
TOY STORY 2
WOW
GROLIER
BOOKS

Andy raced around his room, playing with his two special toys. "You should never tangle with the unstoppable duo of Sheriff Woody and Buzz Lightyear!" Andy said. Suddenly—

RRRIP! Andy accidentally ripped Woody's arm. And Andy was supposed to leave for Cowboy Camp any minute. Would he still take Woody?

Andy's mother suggested they try to fix Woody. But Andy decided to leave Woody home this year.

Andy's mother put Woody high up on a shelf. From there, Woody watched sadly as Andy left.

Andy had never before gone to Cowboy Camp without him. Woody wondered if Andy would forget about him.

The next morning Woody heard a sickly cough next to him on the shelf. It was Wheezy, a little toy penguin.

"Wheezy!" cried Woody. "Where've you been?"

"After my squeaker broke, I was put up here on the shelf and forgotten." Wheezy sighed. "We're all just one stitch away from here to there, anyway," he went on, pointing out the window.

Outside, Andy's mother was setting up a yard sale! She came into Andy's room looking for items for the sale, and she grabbed Wheezy!

Woody sprang into action. He jumped onto Andy's dog, Buster, to rescue the squeakless penguin.

Wheezy made it back to Andy's room with Buster, but Buster didn't see that Woody had fallen off until it was too late.

Suddenly Woody was spotted by a stranger! The man picked up the toy cowboy and clutched him in his greedy hands. "I found him!" he said.

"How much for this stuff?" he asked Andy's mother.

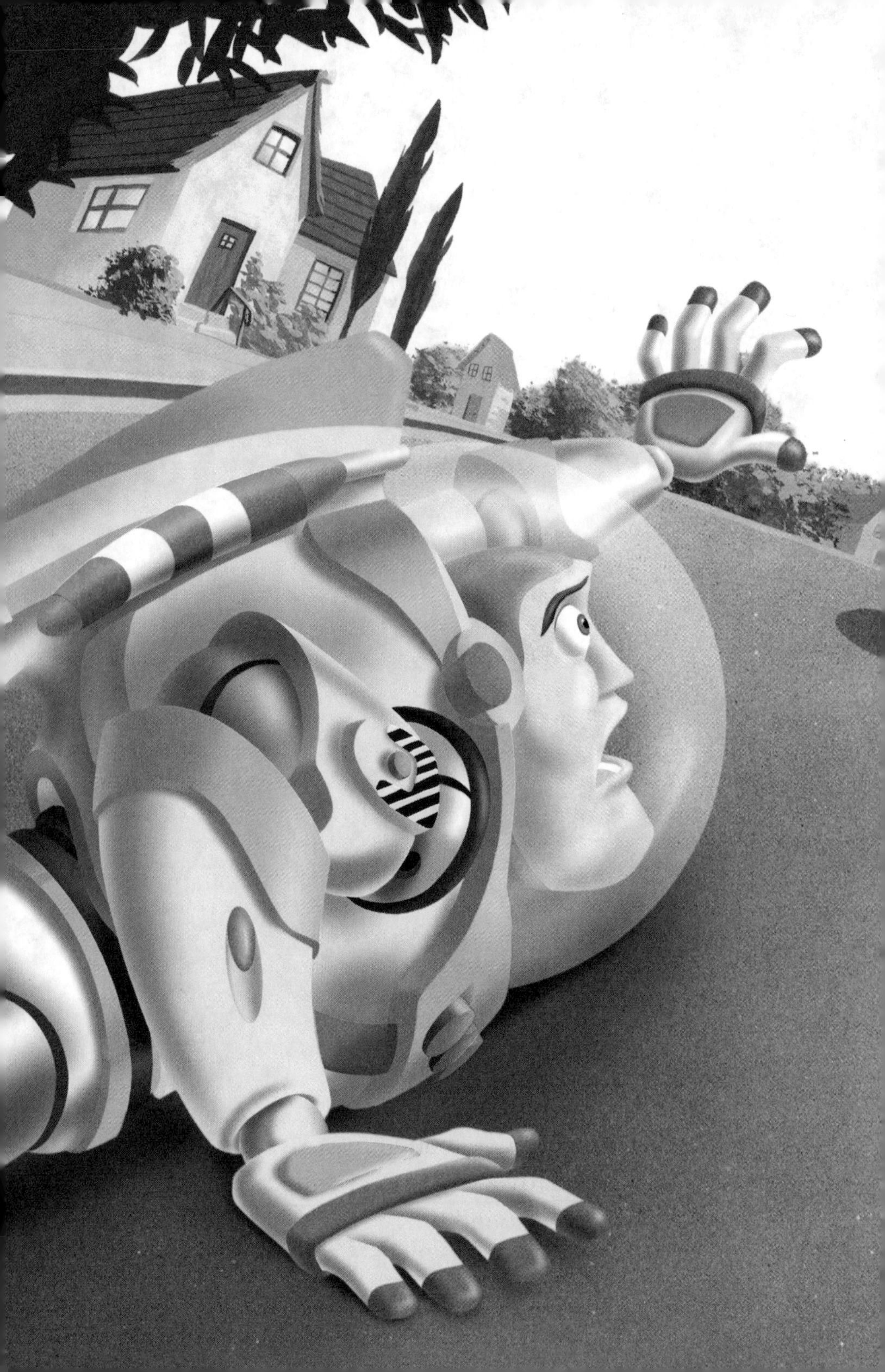

Andy's mother refused to sell Woody. So the stranger snatched him and ran off!

"Oh, no!" cried Buzz Lightyear, watching from Andy's bedroom window. "He's stealing Woody!"

In a flash Buzz leaped out the window and slid down the drainpipe.

But Buzz was too late. The stranger had jumped into his car with Woody and was speeding off. The last thing Buzz saw was the car's license plate, which read "LZTYBRN."

The thief raced back to his home and put Woody in a glass case. Once the man left, Woody opened the case and tried to escape. Suddenly—

"YEEE-HAHHH!"

Three unfamiliar toys surrounded Woody: a cowgirl, a horse, and a prospector—still in his original box.

"It's you! It's really you!" shouted the cowgirl.

The horse eagerly licked Woody's face.

"We've waited countless years for this day, Woody," the Prospector welcomed him, smiling.

"Who are you?" Woody asked, confused. "How do you know my name?"

The toys introduced themselves: Jessie the yodeling cowgirl, Stinky Pete the Prospector, and Bullseye, the sharpest horse in the West! The Prospector explained that they were part of a collection based on a TV show called *Woody's Roundup*. Woody was the star!

"Wow!" exclaimed Woody, watching a videotape of the show. "That's me!"

Meanwhile, Buzz and the rest of the toys learned that the license plate "LZTYBRN" stood for "Al's Toy Barn." The toys knew Al from his TV commercials. It was Al who had stolen Woody!

Buzz outlined a plan to get Woody back.

"Woody once risked his life to save me," Buzz explained. "I couldn't call myself his friend if I wasn't willing to do the same. Who's with me?"

That night, Buzz, Slinky, Mr. Potato Head, Hamm, and Rex set out to rescue their stolen friend. Buzz led the way.

"To Al's Toy Barn—and beyond!" he cried.

Meanwhile, back at Al's, Woody learned it was true. He had once been a TV star.

Al had collected every toy from the show except one—Sheriff Woody.

The Roundup Gang had spent years in a storage box as Al searched for Woody.

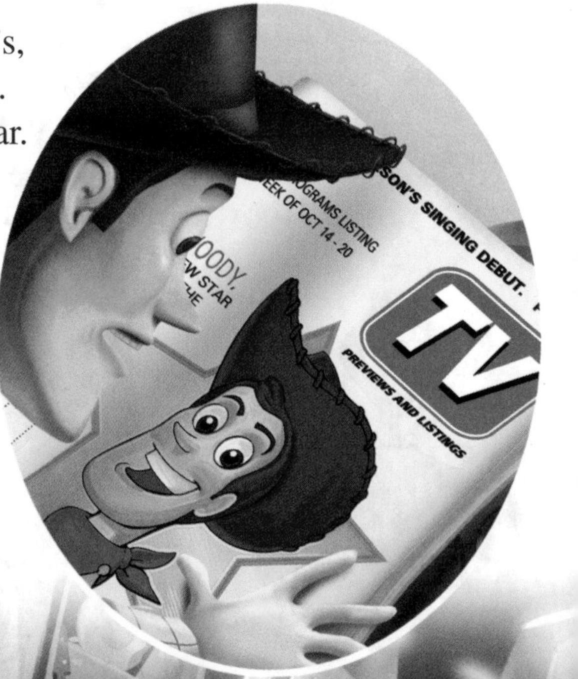

"WOOO-EEE!" howled Jessie. "Look at us! Now we're a complete set!"

Woody, Jessie, and Bullseye started playing with the Roundup toys.

"Now Al can sell us to the museum in Japan," said the Prospector.

"Museum?" asked Woody. "But I've gotta get back home to my owner, Andy."

Jessie was crushed. Without Woody, they would be returned to the storage box.

Then Al returned, and the toys hurried back to their places. They heard Al telephone a toy museum in Japan. The museum agreed to buy the Roundup Gang!

"I promise this collection will be the crown jewel of your museum!" Al guaranteed, hanging up the phone.

The toy collector grabbed Woody out of the case. Oops! Woody's arm got caught and tore off completely.

Al called a man named “the Cleaner” to come and fix Woody. Soon Woody was not just as good as new—he was better than new. The Cleaner even painted over Andy’s name on the bottom of Woody’s shoe.

But it didn’t matter. Woody was still ready to go back home to Andy.

Before he left, Woody stopped to say good-bye to the Roundup Gang. And that’s when Jessie told him about her little girl.

"Andy's your best friend, right?" Jessie asked Woody. "When he plays with you, you feel alive."

"How did you know that?" asked Woody.

"Because my owner, Emily, was just the same. She was my whole world," Jessie told him.

"It's funny," she added, "you *never* forget them, but they forget you. She gave me away when she grew up."

Jessie's words made Woody sad. He was afraid of Andy outgrowing him. He wondered if he should just stay with the Roundup Gang instead of going home.

Meanwhile, it had been a long night for the other toys. The gang had walked and walked to reach Al's Toy Barn.

By morning, they stood across the street from the toy store. But now they had to cross a busy street!

Luckily, Buzz had an idea. The toys hid in traffic cones and ran across the street.

Mr. Potato Head was almost turned into a mashed potato!

Soon, though, they were all safe on the other side.

Buzz and the others slipped inside Al's Toy Barn. They didn't find Woody, but they did meet some interesting toys. Buzz even met another Buzz Lightyear!

Soon, though, the toys found their missing buddy in Al's apartment across the street.

"Woody!" Buzz cried. "You're in danger here. We need to leave now!"

But now Woody didn't want to go.

Woody told his stunned friends about the TV show, the Roundup Gang, and the museum.

"Buzz, you don't understand," Woody tried to explain. "Andy is growing up, and one day he won't need me any longer. This is my chance to last forever in a museum."

"Museum? You want to watch children from behind glass? Some life!" Buzz wailed.

"You are a *toy,* Woody, a child's plaything. You have to be there for Andy! Remember?" Buzz asked. "You taught me that!"

But Woody wouldn't go.

As the other toys from Andy's room sadly left, Woody turned and saw his old TV show. There on the TV set was a boy who looked like Andy. Woody scratched off the paint on his shoe and looked at Andy's name. He knew he'd made a mistake.

"What am I doing?!" Woody shouted.

So what if someday Andy outgrew him! Until then, Woody wanted to spend every single minute with his best friend!

"Buzz! Buzz! Wait!" Woody called out. "I'm coming with you!"

He asked Jessie and Bullseye to come, too.

But the Prospector slipped out of his box and stopped them. "I've waited too long for this!" he said. "You are not going to ruin my plans!"

Before they could get any farther, in came Al!

Al grabbed the Roundup Gang and put them in a case. He was heading for the airport to fly to Japan. There he would sell them to the museum.

Andy's toys raced to save Woody, fearing they might lose him forever! But before they could get him out of the toy case, the Prospector yanked him back inside!

Buzz and the gang ran outside after Al. But Al got into his car and sped off.

"How are we going to get him now?" Rex asked.

Just then Mr. Potato Head spotted a Pizza Planet delivery van. "Pizza, anyone?" he said slyly.

The toys jumped into the vehicle.

"Slink, take the pedals," Buzz commanded. "Rex, you navigate. Hamm and Potato, operate the levers and knobs!"

They raced after Al's car.

When Al reached the airport, he had to check in the toy case. The toys went into the baggage area on a conveyor belt that took the bags out to the planes.

The Roundup Gang was on its way to Japan!

But Buzz and the other toys, hiding in a pet carrier, followed the case into the baggage area.

Buzz flew up to rescue Woody.

The Prospector tried to stop them, but Woody and Buzz managed to put him in a backpack full of dolls.

"You'll like Amy," they said. "She's an artist."

Buzz, Woody, and Bullseye managed to escape. But Jessie was still trapped.

"Woody! Help!" pleaded Jessie as she was loaded onto the plane.

There was only one thing to do. Woody and Buzz jumped onto Bullseye.

"Ride like the wind, Bullseye!" Woody cried as they galloped off to save Jessie.

Woody jumped aboard the plane.

"Come on, Jessie," urged Woody. "It's time to take you home."

"But I'm a girl toy," Jessie moaned. "Andy's not gonna like me."

"Nonsense!" Woody replied. "Andy'll love you! Besides, he's got a little sister."

"He does?!" Jessie answered. "Let's go!"

Suddenly the baggage door closed. The plane started to move!

There was only one way out—an opening just above the landing gear.

“Uh, are you sure about this?” Jessie asked nervously as she climbed down.

“Yes. Now go!” replied Woody, following her. But Woody slipped on the oily gear! He held on with one arm. But it was his bad arm. It started to tear again!

“Hold on, Woody!” Jessie cried.

"Just a minute," a familiar voice called. "You can't have a rescue without Buzz Lightyear!"

"Buzz!" yelled Woody, seeing his old partner atop his new pal Bullseye.

Woody had an idea. He twirled his pull string like a lasso and wrapped it around the landing gear. Woody and Jessie swung away and landed safely on Bullseye.

"Nice ropin', cowboy!" cheered Buzz.

"Now let's all go home," Woody said, grinning.

When Andy came back from camp, he was so anxious to see his toys that he didn't wonder about the airport baggage cart parked in front of his house. He bounded up the stairs to his room. He saw Woody and Buzz and his brand-new Jessie and Bullseye toys.

"Oh, wow! Thanks!" he called downstairs to his mother.

"I'm proud of you, Woody," Buzz said later.

"Thanks, pal," Woody answered. "You know, someday, when it all ends, it's good to know that I'll still have Buzz Lightyear to keep me company for infinity and beyond."

Hey howdy hey!
Woody's
ROUNDUP
Woody's
ROUNDUP
Woody's
ROUNDUP